HURRICANE

HURRICANE

CHRISTOPHER LAMPTON

THE MILLBROOK PRESS
BROOKFIELD, CT
A DISASTER! BOOK

Cover photograph courtesy of the National Weather Service

Illustrations by Pat Scully

Photographs courtesy of Superstock: pp. 6, 12–13, 16, 43, 54–55; National Weather Service: pp. 8, 11, 32–33, 45; National Hurricane Center: pp. 11, 29, 35; NOAA: pp. 14, 47; Science Source Photo Researchers: pp. 21 (Hal Harrison), 48, bottom (Larry Mulvehill), 51, top (Jules Bucher), and bottom; NCAR: p. 26; UPI/Bettmann News-photos: p. 36; Dr. Frank Marks, Hurricane Research Division: p. 48, top; Wide World Photos, Inc.: p. 56.

Cataloging-in-Publication Data
Lampton, Christopher
Hurricane / by Christopher Lampton
p.   cm.—(A Disaster! Book)
Bibliography p.   Includes index.
Summary: Describes a hurricane experience and its destruction. Explains how the weather bureau can detect, measure, predict and warn people about a hurricane experience. Discusses the means of protecting oneself.
ISBN 1-56294-030-9   ISBN 0-395-63643-4 (pbk.)
1. Hurricanes. 2. Typhoons. 3. Meteorology. 4. Storms. I. Title.
II. Series.
551.5   1991

CONTENTS

HURRICANE!

The first sign is a change in the waves. Where once they broke gently against the beach, they are now larger and more violent. They wash farther inland than you have ever seen them go before.

The second sign is in the sky. Dark and gloomy, the clouds start gathering thickly over the ocean. Then they roll inland, blackening the sky. Along with the clouds comes a rising wind. At first, it's no more than a breeze. Then a series of gusts scatters leaves and papers across the ground and over the roofs of buildings.

At last it begins to rain, not just a gentle sprinkle but a powerful torrent. The rain passes quickly, but it is back again in an hour, stronger than ever. The rain is driven by the wind. It pounds against windows like a beating fist. The wind howls between houses, blowing awnings off porches and knocking electrical wires loose from poles.

The waves crash fiercely against the beach. Then, suddenly, there is no more beach! The water rises higher and higher. It covers not just the beach but piers and bridges. Suddenly the ocean is washing past houses and cars. It rushes right down the main street of town, battering against walls and even knocking them down. Automobiles float past your front door.

Windows are shattered by the sheer force of the winds. Panes of glass are lifted into the air and hurled like Frisbees. They slice through anything that gets in their way.

Violent waves crashing against the shore cover houses and piers.

You are in the middle of a hurricane, the biggest storm on earth and one of the most destructive forces known to humankind. It's not a very safe place to be. If you had been smart, you would have heeded the warnings issued by the Weather Bureau hours earlier and left town. But now you are huddled inside what is left of your home as it is battered by the sea.

Finally, the storm ceases. The winds grow calm and you hear the sound of birds crying in the air. You step out of your house and look around. The street is littered with debris such as tree limbs and pools of water. Although rays of sunlight are beginning to break through overhead, there is a wall of dark clouds surrounding you. As you watch the clouds, they seem to move around you in a slow circle.

You are inside the eye of the storm. Although it seems as if the storm has passed, it is really only half over. The second half of the storm is on its way, and it will be every bit as bad as the first half!

You re-enter your house and batten down the hatches once more. With luck, you'll still be there in the morning, when the storm is gone. You won't become part of the debris that is about to be swept away into the sea around you!

HURRICANES EVERY YEAR

Hurricanes are a natural phenomenon that occur every year, at around the same time. In the eastern United States, hurricane season starts in late June and lasts until late December, although most hurricanes occur in late summer and fall. Fortunately, most hurricanes (and tropical storms, which are similar but less destructive) fizzle out before they reach land. Some strike in unpopulated regions where they can't cause much damage to houses and other buildings.

But storms don't come any bigger than the biggest hurricanes, and every few years one of them turns its full force on a heavily populated region. The result is disaster! Here are a few of the hurricanes that have been especially destructive in years past:

■ In 1900, an unnamed hurricane entered the Gulf of Mexico. It came ashore at Galveston, an island city just off the southern coast of Texas. The bridge that connected Galveston with the mainland disappeared under the water, cutting off the only evacuation route. Waves as tall as 5 feet rushed through the city,

■ 10

Hurricane Hugo wreaked havoc in the Virgin Islands, Puerto Rico, and along the South Atlantic coast, particularly Charleston (above), in September 1989.

tearing down hundreds of buildings. By the next morning, 10,000 people had died in Galveston and the surrounding area.

■ Hurricane Camille struck the Mississippi Delta on August 17, 1969. Waves 20 feet tall knocked down buildings. They swept through cities along the Mississippi coast and swallowed entire

bridges around New Orleans. When the storm was over, high-ways were buried under sand. Hundreds of miles of road could not be used. Approximately $1.5 million worth of damage had been done. Fortunately, the area had been evacuated before the storm. Only 250 people were killed.

Damage from Hurricane Camille in the Mississippi Delta.

Hurricane Frederic was the costliest hurricane in U.S. history.

■ On November 12, 1979, Hurricane Frederic became the costliest hurricane in U.S. history. It battered Mobile Bay, Alabama, with 144-mile-per-hour (mph) winds and flooded Gulf Shore, Alabama, to a depth of 14 feet. It traveled as far north as Maine before disappearing into the Atlantic Ocean. In the process, it caused $2.3 billion in damage.

■ One area far from the North Atlantic that has been particularly hard hit by hurricanes from the Indian Ocean is the tiny country of Bangladesh. This country is built on low-lying land, and many of its citizens live close to the ocean. A single storm surge can take thousands of Bangladeshi lives. In 1971, a hurricane killed 300,000 people in Bangladesh. More recently, a 1991 hurricane there took at least 150,000 lives.

What causes hurricanes? Why does nature suddenly turn deadly, spawning a storm that can destroy entire towns and take thousands of lives in a few hours?

To answer that question, we'll have to talk for a moment about weather in general. And we'll have to look at the way in which hot air and water can cause storms.

Clouds are formed of water droplets floating in the air.

HOW CLOUDS FORM

If you live in a two-story house, you've probably noticed that the rooms upstairs tend to be warmer than the rooms downstairs. That's because hot air rises. Centuries ago, balloonists took advantage of this principle by filling their balloons with hot air so that they could soar high into the clouds.

Why does hot air rise? Air is made of tiny particles, called *molecules.* These molecules become excited when they are heated. This causes them to move farther apart. This, in turn, makes the warm air lighter and less dense than the colder air around it. The colder air sinks down and pushes the warm air up, like bubbles rising in water.

Air is made up of many different kinds of molecules. Some of them are molecules of water, in a form called *water vapor.* Water vapor is an invisible gas. It is always present in all but the driest of air. Water molecules enter the air when the air passes over water. The hottest water molecules in the water become excited and literally jump out of the water into the air, becoming water vapor.

How Warm Air Rises

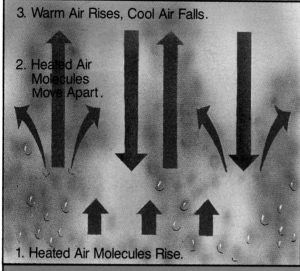

3. Warm Air Rises, Cool Air Falls.

2. Heated Air Molecules Move Apart.

1. Heated Air Molecules Rise.

Air molecules become excited when they are heated, causing them to move apart. This makes the warm air less dense than the colder air around it. The colder air sinks down, pushing the warm air up.

How Clouds Form

Some of the molecules in the air are water vapor. As the water vapor in warm air rises, it forms clouds. Cooler air turns the water vapor in clouds into droplets of water. When these water droplets become heavy, they fall to the ground as rain.

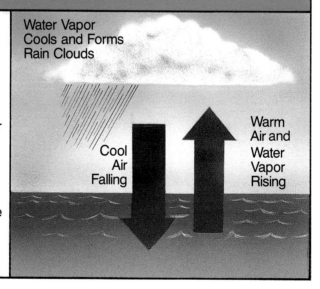

Water Vapor Cools and Forms Rain Clouds

Cool Air Falling

Warm Air and Water Vapor Rising

Ironically, air becomes cooler as it rises. When the rising air reaches a certain height above the ground, it becomes so cool that the water vapor in the air *condenses.* That is, it turns back into droplets of water. These droplets are so small, however, that they float in the air without falling back to earth. On most days, you can look up in the sky and see billions of these water droplets floating in the air. You call them *clouds.*

Occasionally, these water droplets will come together to form larger droplets, which are too heavy to float in the air. They then fall out of the cloud and become rain. Because the air high above the ground is very cold—below freezing temperature—these droplets often begin their journey to the ground in frozen form. If the air near the ground is warm, they melt into raindrops. Otherwise, they reach the ground as snow, sleet, or hail.

HIGH- AND LOW-PRESSURE AREAS

When a lot of air is rising over one area of the earth's surface, we say that it is a *low-pressure* area. This is because the rising air doesn't press down very hard on the ground below. Low-pressure areas tend to be cloudy. And they tend to have a lot of rain and snow, because the rising air carries a great deal of water vapor upward.

Areas where the air is falling are called *high-pressure* areas. This is because the falling air presses down harder on the ground below. High-pressure areas tend to be clear and sunny. There is no rising air to carry water vapor upward to form clouds.

The air pressure where you live changes all the time. Areas of high and low pressure appear and then disappear or move around from place to place. You can measure the pressure of the air around you by using a device called a *barometer.* A barometer is literally a scale for weighing the air. The "heavier" the surrounding air is, the higher the air pressure. The "lighter" the surrounding air is, the lower the air pressure.

The weight of the air is called the *barometric pressure.* If the barometer shows that the barometric pressure is rising, then the weather will probably be fair. If the barometric pressure is falling, then the weather will probably be cloudy.

When air rises in a low-pressure area, the air near the ground is quickly replaced by air from someplace else. The air that replaces the rising air comes from the nearest high-pressure zone, in the form of a brisk wind. You've probably noticed that some days are extremely windy. The wind blows for hours on end. That means you're right between a high-pressure area and a low-pressure area. The wind is blowing from the high-pressure area to replace the rising air in the low-pressure area.

Barometers measure rising and falling air.

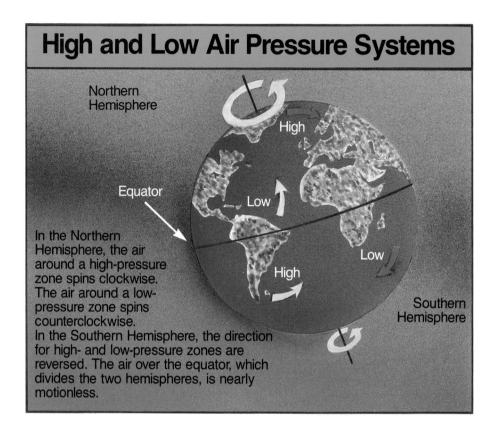

High and Low Air Pressure Systems

Northern Hemisphere

High

Equator

Low

In the Northern Hemisphere, the air around a high-pressure zone spins clockwise. The air around a low-pressure zone spins counterclockwise. In the Southern Hemisphere, the direction for high- and low-pressure zones are reversed. The air over the equator, which divides the two hemispheres, is nearly motionless.

High

Low

Southern Hemisphere

This tells us something important about high- and low-pressure areas. Air is always moving *into* a low-pressure area and *out of* a high-pressure area. But the air doesn't move *straight* in and out. Remember that the planet earth underneath all of this air is rotating on its own axis. This rotation gives the moving air a twist that actually sets it spinning in a large spiral around the high- and low-pressure areas.

In the Northern Hemisphere, the air around a high-pressure area spins clockwise. The air around a low-pressure area spins counterclockwise. In the Southern Hemisphere, these directions for high- and low-pressure areas are reversed. The air over the equator, which divides the two hemispheres, doesn't spin at all.

TROPICAL DEPRESSIONS

The heat that causes air to rise comes from the sun. In fact, most of the heat on earth comes from the sun. Because the earth is a sphere, some parts of it get more heat from the sun than others. Most of the heat from the sun falls on the region around the equator. The least heat falls on the North and South poles.

As you might guess, the air at the equator tends to be quite warm. This air is almost always rising. It tends to rain a lot at the equator, for just this reason. As we pointed out in the last section, the air rushing into this low-pressure zone doesn't spin because it is located right on the equator.

In late summer, however, low-pressure areas will sometimes form in the ocean just to the north of the equator. This frequently happens in the Atlantic Ocean, for instance, off the western coast of Africa. Because these low-pressure areas are not directly on the equator, the wind rushing into them will spin in a counterclockwise direction. This is just like in any other low-pressure area in the

Northern Hemisphere. Such low-pressure areas close to the equator are called *tropical depressions.*

The water near the equator receives a lot of heat from the sun. This creates a lot of water vapor. The water vapor rises in the air and forms clouds in a tropical depression. It carries the sun's heat upward with it as it rises. When it condenses into water droplets, it releases that heat into the air. This makes the air even hotter, which causes it to rise even faster.

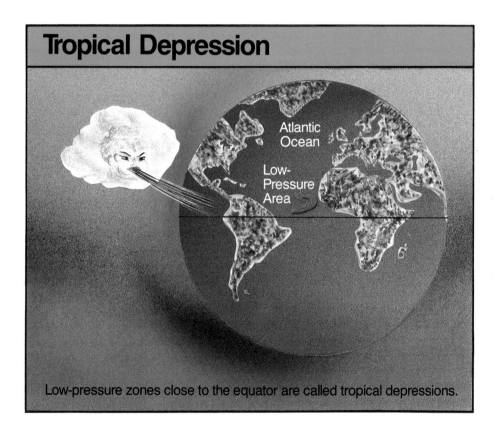

Tropical Depression

Atlantic Ocean

Low-Pressure Area

Low-pressure zones close to the equator are called tropical depressions.

This rising air acts like a giant suction pump. It sucks more air up beneath it. This air, in turn, carries still more water vapor that releases still more heat when it condenses. The air rises faster and faster. The wind rushes in to replace this air, and the low-pressure area spins faster and faster. When the tropical depression begins to sustain winds with an average speed of at least 39 mph, it stops being a tropical depression. It becomes a *tropical storm.*

Cumulonimbus, or rain-producing, clouds form as moisture in updrafts condenses. When the droplets in the clouds become too heavy, the rain falls out of the cloud. Note in this picture the rainshaft at right.

FROM TROPICAL STORM TO HURRICANE

Far above the earth, meteorological (weather) satellites take pictures of the swirling clouds that mark the tropical storm. They beam these pictures back to meteorologists (weather forecasters) on the ground. The tropical storm is given a name and is watched carefully to see what it does next.

Many tropical storms simply die out, never to be heard from again. But others grow stronger. The winds blow faster and faster as more and more air containing hot water vapor is sucked up into the clouds. When the winds in the tropical storm average more than 75 mph, it becomes a *hurricane.*

Whether it's a tropical storm or a hurricane, the storm almost always will begin moving west, toward the Americas. It moves west because the winds over the Atlantic Ocean, which sailors of old called the "trade winds," almost always blow west. They blow west for the same reason that air in a low-pressure area spins counter-clockwise—because the earth is rotating west to east underneath them.

This striking satellite image of Hurricane Hugo was recorded at 6 p.m. on September 21, 1989.

Many such storms will simply continue moving west. Others will "recurve" to the north. If the storms don't die out, they will eventually reach land. Sometimes they will strike at the many islands in the Caribbean Sea. Sometimes they will enter the Gulf of Mexico. And other times they will head north until they hit land somewhere along the east coast of the United States.

When they reach land, these storms can cause great destruction. Fortunately, once the storm "comes ashore," it will rapidly lose its main source of power—the warm seawater that supplies the water vapor for the storm. But before it loses its full power, it can wreak havoc in inhabited areas along the shoreline.

HURRICANE DESTRUCTION

We mentioned earlier that air pressure is the pressure with which the air is pressing down on the ground—and on you, as well. You don't usually notice this pressure because your body has adapted to it. At greater altitudes above the ground, there is less air pressure, because there is less air to press down. Sometimes, when you go up in an airplane or drive to the top of a mountain in a car, you notice the sudden drop in air pressure. The inside of your ear begins to feel clogged until your body adapts to the lower air pressure.

The air pressure inside a hurricane is very low. In fact, it is lower than the air pressure ever gets under normal conditions. As the pressure goes down, the ocean underneath the hurricane actually rises. In fact, the water can rise several feet above normal.

Meteorologists refer to this increase in the water level as a *storm surge.* It is the greatest single destructive force in a hurricane. It is even greater than the 200 mph winds and the crashing waves. Of every ten people who die in a hurricane, nine are killed by the storm surge!

When the storm surge reaches the shore, it can rise even higher. Slowed down by the land, the high waters can pile up. They can cause the water level to increase in height by as much as 25 feet above normal! This was the case in Pass Christian, Mississippi, during the 1969 hurricane Camille.

In a storm surge, domes of water 40 to 50 miles across can sweep the coastline.

Sometimes the storm surge comes on gradually. The water level rises over several hours. But at other times it can happen all at once. In those cases the water rises in minutes, even seconds.

If this happens in a coastal town, the streets can suddenly be flooded by high waters. Cars and even buildings can be swept away.

People, caught by surprise, can drown before they are able to reach high ground. Islands and bridges can disappear completely under the waters for hours.

The famous Galveston flood in the 1900 hurricane was caused by a storm surge. A storm surge in India's Ganges River in 1970 killed hundreds of thousands of people! The storm surge in Hurricane Camille completely covered the world's longest bridge. The Lake Pontchartrain causeway, north of New Orleans, was covered for several hours.

The storm surge is not the only destructive force in a hurricane, though. Hurricane winds commonly blow at speeds of more than 100 mph. Many hurricanes have winds as high as 200 mph. Although it is difficult to measure winds of this intensity and higher, meteorologists believe that hurricane winds can go as high as 250 mph.

Winds of this force can blow down buildings. They can turn ordinary objects into deadly weapons by hurling them through the air at speeds high enough to kill on impact.

The rains produced by a hurricane can cause severe flooding. As much as 5 to 15 inches of rain can fall in a few hours. Hurricane Dennis, in 1981, dropped 20 inches of rain on Florida in a single day.

Hurricanes lose their force quickly after they come onto land. However, they can cause flooding over great distances inland. Hurricane Hazel in 1954 caused flooding from the Carolinas, where it came ashore, all the way to the Great Lakes. The next year, Hurricane Diane caused more than a billion dollars worth of flood damage.

The waves produced by a hurricane can also cause considerable damage. This is true even when there is no storm surge. They

Hurricanes can turn cars into deadly weapons.

can rise to heights of 60 feet or greater; hurricane waves as tall as 90 feet have been reported in a few unusual instances.

Hurricane waves not only destroy buildings and other structures on the shore. They can also wash away the shore itself, destroying beachfront property worth millions of dollars. The waves don't even necessarily accompany the hurricane. They can arrive before the storm or after it's gone. And they can strike portions of the shore far from the hurricane itself.

This view of Fire Island in New York shows expensive beachfront property reduced to matchwood by a hurricane.

NAMING HURRICANES

No one is quite sure when the practice of naming tropical storms and hurricanes began. In the beginning, only those storms that had caused an unusually large amount of damage were named, and these names were purely informal. Some historians have suggested that the first person to give names systematically to weather systems was the Australian meteorologist Clement Wragge early in the twentieth century. Wragge named high-pressure areas after his friends and low-pressure areas after his enemies.

The modern practice of naming hurricanes, however, did not begin until World War II. It might have been inspired by the best-selling novel *Storm* (1941) by George Stewart. In that book, meteorologists named hurricanes after their girlfriends, famous figures, and so forth. In 1953, the practice of giving hurricanes female names in alphabetical order was officially established. From 1979 on, male names were alternated with female names.

Every so often, a list of names is decided on. This list is then distributed to meteorologists. (Different lists are distributed in each of the tropical storm-producing areas of the world. This is to distinguish between the storms produced by each.) The first hurricane of the year is given a name beginning with A, the second a name beginning with B, the third a name beginning with C, and so on. For example, if the first is named Alan, the second might be named Betty, and the third Carl. There aren't many names beginning with Q, U, X, Y, and Z, so those letters aren't used for hurricanes in the Atlantic Ocean and the western Pacific Ocean. (Names beginning with X, Y, and Z *are* used in the eastern Pacific.) However, the letters past O are rarely needed anyway.

Following (Figure 1) is the list of the names used for hurricanes in the Atlantic Ocean in the years 1985 through 1994. Notice how the names repeat every six years. However, the list is periodically revised so that the names of particularly violent storms can be "retired," much like the number of a famous sports figure is retired when he or she leaves the sport. Following this list are lists of the names used in the eastern Pacific Ocean (Figure 2) and in the western Pacific Ocean (Figure 3). Notice that the names in the western Pacific are repeated every four years, without regard to year.

HURRICANE NAMES

FIGURE 1: ATLANTIC

1985 Ana, Bob, Claudette, David, Elena, Fabian, Gloria, Henri, Isabel, Juan, Kate, Larry, Mindy, Nicholas, Odette, Peter, Rose, Sam, Theresa, Victor, Wanda.

1986 Andrew, Bonnie, Charley, Danielle, Earl, Frances, Georges, Hermine, Ivan, Jeanne, Karl, Lisa, Mitch, Nicole, Otto, Paula, Richard, Shary, Tomas, Virginie, Walter.

1987 Arlene, Bret, Cindy, Dennis, Emily, Floyd, Gert, Harvey, Irene, Jose, Katrina, Lenny, Maria, Nate, Ophellia, Phillippe, Rita, Stan, Tammy, Vince, Wilma.

1988 Alberto, Beryl, Chris, Debby, Ernesto, Florence, Gilbert, Helene, Issac, Joan, Keith, Leslie, Michael, Nadine, Oscar, Patty, Raphael, Sandy, Tony, Valerie, William.

1989 Allison, Barry, Chantal, Dean, Erin, Felix, Gabrielle, Hugo, Iris, Jerry, Karen, Luis, Marilyn, Noel, Opal, Pablo, Roxanne, Sebastien, Tanya, Van, Wendy.

1990 Arthur, Bertha, Cesar, Diana, Edouard, Fran, Gustav, Hortense, Isidore, Josephine, Klaus, Lili, Marco, Nana, Omar, Paloma, Rene, Sally, Teddy, Vicky, Wilfred.

1991 Ana, Bob, Claudette, David, Elena, Fabian, Gloria, Henri, Isabel, Juan, Kate, Larry, Mindy, Nicholas, Odette, Peter, Rose, Sam, Theresa, Victor, Wanda.

1992 Andrew, Bonnie, Charley, Danielle, Earl, Frances, Georges, Hermine, Ivan, Jeanne, Karl, Lisa, Mitch, Nicole, Otto, Paula, Richard, Shary, Tomas, Virginie, Walter.

1993 Arlene, Bret, Cindy, Dennis, Emily, Floyd, Gert, Harvey, Irene, Jose, Katrina, Lenny, Maria, Nate, Ophellia, Phillippe, Rita, Stan, Tammy, Vince, Wilma.

1994 Alberto, Beryl, Chris, Debby, Ernesto, Florence, Gilbert, Helene, Issac, Joan, Keith, Leslie, Michael, Nadine, Oscar, Patty, Raphael, Sandy, Tony, Valerie, William.

FIGURE 2: EASTERN PACIFIC

1986 Agatha, Blas, Celia, Darby, Estelle, Frank, Georgette, Howard, Isis, Javier, Kay, Lester, Madeline, Newton, Oriene, Paine, Roslyn, Seymour, Tina, Virgil, Winifred, Xavier, Yolanda, Zeke.

1987 Adrian, Beatriz, Calvin, Dora, Eugene, Fernanda, Greg, Hilary, Irwin, Jova, Knut, Lidia, Max, Norma, Otis, Pilar, Ramon, Selma, Todd, Veronica, Wiley, Xina, York, Zelda.

1988 Aletta, Bud, Carlotta, Daniel, Emilia, Fabio, Gilma, Hector, Iva, John, Kristy, Lane, Miriam, Norman, Olivia, Paul, Rosa, Sergio, Tara, Vincente, Willa, Xavier, Yolanda, Zeke.

1989 Adolph, Barbara, Cosme, Dalilia, Erick, Flossie, Gil, Henriette, Ismael, Juliette, Kiko, Lorena, Manuel, Narda, Octave, Priscilla, Raymond, Sonia, Tico, Velma, Winnie, Xina, York, Zelda.

1990 Alma, Boris, Christina, Douglas, Wlida, Fausto, Genevieve, Hernan, Iselle, Julio, Kenna, Lowell, Marie, Norbert, Odile, Polo, Rachel, Simon, Trudy, Vance, Wallis, Xavier, Yolanda, Zeke.

1991 Andres, Blanca, Carlos, Dolores, Enrique, Fefa, Guillermo, Hilda, Ignacio, Jimena, Kevin, Linda, Marty, Nora, Olaf, Pauline, Rick, Sandra, Terry, Vivian, Waldo, Xina, York, Zelda.

FIGURE 3: WESTERN PACIFIC

I Andy, Brenda, Cecil, Dot, Ellis, Faye, Gordon, Hope, Irving, Judy, Ken, Lola, Mac, Nancy, Owen, Peggy, Roger, Sarah, Tip, Vera, Wayne.

II Abby, Ben, Carmen, Dom, Ellen, Forrest, Georgia, Herbert, Ida, Joe, Kim, Lex, Marge, Norris, Orchid, Percy, Ruth, Sperry, Thelma, Vernon, Wynn.

III Alex, Betty, Cary, Dinah, Ed, Freda, Gerald, Holly, Ian, June, Kelly, Lynn, Maury, Nina, Ogden, Phyllis, Roy, Susan, Thad, Vanessa, Warren.

IV Agnes, Bill, Clara, Doyle, Elsie, Fabian, Gay, Hal, Irma, Jeff, Kit, Lee, Mamie, Nelson, Odessa, Pat, Ruby, Skip, Tess, Val, Wynona.

HURRICANES AROUND THE WORLD

The North Atlantic Ocean isn't the only place where hurricanes occur. These are the hurricanes most likely to strike the United States, though. There are also hurricanes in the North and South Pacific and in the Indian Ocean near Australia. (Oddly, there are no hurricanes in the South Atlantic Ocean.)

These other storms are not called hurricanes, however. In the Pacific, they are called *typhoons.* In the Indian Ocean, they are called *cyclones.* Some Australians refer to them as *willy-willies.*

But they are all basically the same kind of storm. The chief difference between them is that those in the Northern Hemisphere rotate in a counterclockwise direction, while those in the Southern Hemisphere rotate in a clockwise direction.

A hurricane bends palm trees in Fiji in June 1990.

THE EYE OF
THE STORM

Viewed from above, a hurricane is a great spiral of clouds. It spins counterclockwise (clockwise in the Southern Hemisphere) and stretches for many hundreds of miles.

But in the middle of the storm there is a hole. This hole is an area usually 20 to 40 miles across that is completely calm. It is called the *eye* of the hurricane.

When the eye passes over an area, the storm seems to come to an abrupt halt. The wind and rain cease. Blue sky breaks through the clouds. The danger seems to have passed. But these calm conditions are misleading. Once the eye has passed, the storm will begin again.

If you don't know anything about hurricanes, you might think that the storm had moved on and then returned. A careful observer, however, would notice something odd. The winds were blowing in one direction before the calm. But they are blowing in a different direction afterward. Imagine that the hurricane is approaching from the east. The first winds would come from the north as the hurricane rotated in a counterclockwise direction. But after the eye had passed, the winds would come from the south.

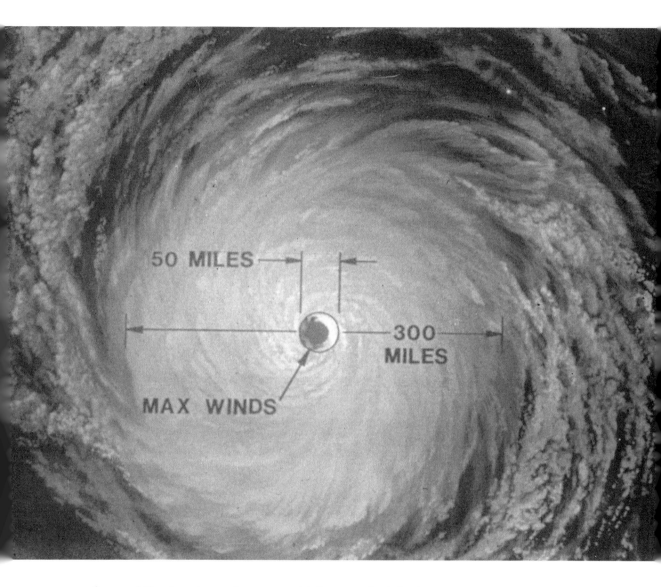

Around the hurricane's eye swirl the most violent winds. Most devastation from a hurricane occurs in the 50 or so mile "doughnut" area around the eye.

PREDICTING HURRICANES

It's not yet possible for us to stop hurricanes. However, it is possible for us to predict them. Areas that are about to be hit by a particularly violent storm can be warned. They can then be evacuated in advance so that the number of deaths can be kept low. That's why very high death tolls—such as the 10,000 lost in Galveston, Texas, in 1900—have been rather rare in storms of this century. Many of the major storms that have struck the United States lately have taken almost no lives at all. This is thanks to advance predictions of the storms' paths.

The first spotters of hurricanes are the weather satellites, most of them placed in orbit by the National Oceanographic and Atmospheric Administration (NOAA). These satellites orbit many thousands of miles above the earth's surface and send pictures to meteorologists below. The satellites can identify tropical storms while they are still forming. They can also monitor their movements as they approach populated coastlines.

The National Hurricane Center in Miami keeps the closest watch on hurricanes. The center maintains a number of weather radar devices in the area between Florida and Texas. When a storm has been sighted, planes are sent into the eye of the storm to measure the speed of the winds. The National Meteorological Center in Maryland, a thousand miles away, uses high-speed computers to sort through the information reported by weather radar devices and tracking planes to try to predict the future of the storm.

A weather satellite placed in orbit by NOAA.

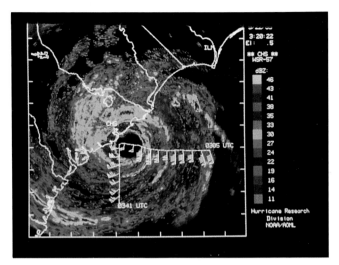

The National Hurricane Center in Miami uses radar and research aircraft to track the progress of Hurricane Hugo over the city of Charleston.

Meteorologists must follow a storm's progress carefully in order to try to predict its ultimate destination.

Unfortunately, even a carefully monitored storm can make un-expected moves. We don't know why, for instance, some hurricanes that form in the North Atlantic move continuously to the west and others suddenly veer to the north. But this sudden change in direction can make a big difference as to where the hurricane strikes. And this, in turn, determines which areas should be evacuated. North Atlantic hurricanes tend to strike in the Caribbean and around the Gulf of Mexico. Some storms, however, can head as far north as New England before going ashore. Meteorologists must watch a storm on a minute-by-minute basis. That's the only way to determine precisely where it is going to head.

Some hurricanes can remain over the same area for several days at a time. They might wreak havoc on a single island or beachfront community. Others will mysteriously vanish before they can cause any destruction at all. And a few may reappear just as mysteriously after vanishing.

It is this kind of unpredictable behavior that frustrates meteorologists who specialize in hurricane prediction. But we must attempt to predict the behavior of these savage storms. Otherwise we will pay too high a cost in human lives.

HURRICANE WARNINGS

When meteorologists spot a hurricane, they immediately start issuing warnings to let people know if the storm is heading their way.

If you live near the shore in an area where hurricanes sometimes strike, you should know how to interpret the hurricane warnings that you hear on the radio or see on television. There are several levels of hurricane warnings, and every one means something different.

If there's a *small-craft warning* in effect, you need not worry unless you are in a boat at sea. This simply means that a hurricane will be passing a few hundred miles from shore and the waves may become too rough for small boats. If you are in a small boat, get to shore as soon as possible!

A *gale warning* means that sharp winds are expected, but not winds of hurricane force. Expect winds of between 38 and 55 mph. If the winds are stronger than a gale, in the range of 55 to 74 mph, a *storm warning* will be issued. In both cases, a hurricane may be nearby, but it isn't expected to hit you directly. This forecast can change suddenly, though.

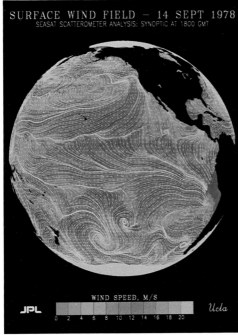

SURFACE WIND FIELD — 14 SEPT 1978
SEASAT SCATTEROMETER ANALYSIS: SYNOPTIC AT 1800 GMT

WIND SPEED, M/S

JPL   0 2 4 6 8 10 12 14 16 18 20   Ucla

Above: *An instrument called an anemometer, connected to this weather vane, measures the speed of the wind, helping meteorologists to forecast changes in the weather.* Left: *Global wind speeds are shown here in different colors. Blue indicates winds of 2 to 9 mph; gray 9 to 13 mph; red 13 to 35 mph; and yellow 35 to 43 mph. The data was obtained from NASA's Seasat satellite.*

A *hurricane watch* means that a hurricane is a possibility, but it won't happen right away. Listen to your radio or TV for further information and start taking advance precautions (see next section). But there's no need to evacuate the area yet.

If a hurricane is on its way and should hit your area within the next 24 hours, a *hurricane warning* is issued. This is the time to take action!

But what sort of action should you take?

IN CASE OF
A HURRICANE

If the hurricane is expected to be fairly severe and you live close to the shore, there's a good chance that you will be asked to evacuate the area. If this request comes from city officials, don't think twice about evacuating. Do it! As we've said earlier, hurricanes are the most powerful storms on earth, and they can kill! You don't want to be around when a hurricane strikes with its full force. Sitting out a hurricane may sound like fun, but it isn't. It's dangerous and frightening! And even if you aren't harmed in the storm, you may find yourself sitting around for days without electric power or running water, which isn't anybody's idea of fun.

Even if you aren't asked to evacuate by local authorities, you can decide to evacuate on your own. If you live directly on the Atlantic Ocean or the Gulf of Mexico, this might be a wise course of action. If you live in a trailer or mobile home, you may also want to evacuate. Houses alongside rivers not far from the coast can also be in peril during a storm. But that's a decision that you or other members of your family will have to make. If you are not

directly on the water and you live in a house on high ground, you may be in a position to ride out the storm.

When you hear that a hurricane watch is in effect, make sure that your family car has gas in it, in case you have to evacuate unexpectedly. (Don't count on buying gas after a hurricane warning has been issued; lines at the service station may wrap around the block—if the service station is open at all!) Stock up on emergency

Coastal areas particularly suffer from the effects of a hurricane. Shown here is flooding in the city of Triumph, Louisiana, after Hurricane Camille.

supplies, such as medicines and first-aid kits. Buy canned foods in case you're stuck in your house for a long period of time. Put fresh batteries in your flashlights, in case the lights go out, and in your portable radios, so you can listen to emergency broadcasts in the absence of power. Tie down anything that is loose or might blow away, or put it in the basement or garage. Tape up your windows or close your shutters to avoid broken glass.

And when a hurricane warning is issued, decide whether or not you need to evacuate—and if you do, get going! Make sure all family members and pets are accounted for, and don't let anybody go out into the storm. If you decide to stay home, stock up on fresh water; fill up the bathtub so that you'll have a large emergency supply. Move all people and valuables to the side of the house *away* from the wind, to avoid blowing debris. And if you have to evacuate, do it as soon as possible; don't wait around until the storm actually hits!

When it's all over, life can start getting back to normal. If you had to evacuate, go back home—but be cautious! There may be downed electrical power lines or broken gas mains. Report any problems immediately to the proper authorities.

Evacuating residents leave 1988's Hurricane Gilbert an unwelcoming message on their boarded-up windows.

GLOSSARY

air pressure—the pressure (or weight) with which air presses down on the ground below it.

barometer—a device for measuring air pressure; literally, a scale for weighing the air.

barometric pressure—the air pressure as measured by a barometer.

cloud—a collection of water droplets suspended in the air.

cyclone—a term used for hurricane-like storms in the Indian Ocean.

eye—the central portion of a hurricane, where the storm lets up and all is calm.

high-pressure area—an area where the air is pressing down on the ground with more weight than usual.

hurricane—a tropical depression in which winds are moving faster than 75 mph; the term *hurricane* is generally used only for those storms that originate in the Atlantic Ocean just north of the equator.

low-pressure area—an area where the air is pressing down on the ground with less weight than usual.

meteorological satellite—a satellite that takes photos of weather systems and sends them back to meteorologists on earth in a television signal; also known as *weather satellites.*

meteorologists—scientists who study weather.

molecules—the tiny particles of which air and most other substances are made. Molecules, in turn, are made of atoms.

storm surge—a rise in water level caused by the drop in air pressure in a hurricane, responsible for most of the severe flooding during the storm.

tropical depression—a low-pressure area close to the equator, usually over the ocean.

tropical storm—a tropical depression in which the winds are moving faster than 39 mph but slower than 75 mph.

typhoon—the term used for hurricane-like storms in the Pacific Ocean.

water vapor—an invisible gas made of molecules of water.

willy-willies—an Australian term for hurricane-like storms.

RECOMMENDED READING

Brindze, Ruth. *Monster Storms From the Sea.* New York: Atheneum, 1983.

Erickson, John. *Violent Storms.* Blue Ridge Summit, PA: Tab Books, 1988.

Gibilisco, Stan. *Violent Weather: Hurricanes, Tornadoes and Storms.* Blue Ridge Summit, PA: Tab Books, 1984.

Lambert, David, and Ralph Henry. *Weather and Its Work.* New York: Facts on File, 1984.

Pettigrew, Mark. *Weather.* New York: Gloucester Press, 1987.

Webster, Vera. *Weather Experiments.* Chicago: Children's Press, 1982.

INDEX